LiLi M. Gree

There is no one Like you

Present for girls

Table of content

You Are Unique

Introduction

Dear Girl,
As you embark on your journey with the heroines of this book,
I want you to know just how special and amazing you are!
You are one of a kind, with your own talents and passions
that make you shine. There is no one else in the world exactly
like you, and that is something to celebrate!

Within this book, you will meet other girls who face
challenges and overcome them with determination and
strength. Sometimes it can be scary to try new things or be
different from others, but always remember that being
unique is what makes you special. You have the power to
change the world in your own way, and this book will help
inspire you to do just that.

These stories will encourage you to embrace your
individuality, love yourself for who you are, and show
kindness and support to those around you. So let's embark
on this adventure together and discover the amazing things
that can happen when we believe in ourselves and follow our
hearts!

I Love You

Ari was a little girl who lived in the Kingdom of Mertina. Ari loved spending time with her grandmother. Of course, she loved everyone in her family, but she secretly liked Grandma the most. They spent time together every single day.

Grandma liked to play card games with Ari, and she taught her how to bake cookies. Ari loved her Grandma very much. During the afternoon, Ari liked to play in the garden while her grandmother tended to the Iriss. Ari learned a lot from her Grandmother every single day.

One day, Ari found something in a secluded corner of a quiet garden. Nestled among the vibrant blooms and gently swaying branches, there sat a hurt little bird. Its delicate frame was adorned with feathers of subdued colors, once bright but now dulled by the weight of its pain. From time to time, the bird emitted soft, sad chirps.

Ari wanted to go pick it up, but her grandmother told her not to. Soon, Ari could hear a faint chirping echo through the meadow. Another bird, with feathers shimmering like a cascading rainbow, descended from

the heavens. With cautious steps, it approached the hurt little bird. The newcomer's melodic trills bring solace to the injured bird's weary heart, a soothing balm to its wounded soul. With gentle nudges and reassuring gestures, the savior bird conveyed an unspoken promise of healing and companionship. The hurt little bird began to look up. Even though it shook, it began to try to stand up. The stronger bird offered a branch for its new friend to hold on to. Finally, the injured creature found the strength to rise again. Even though it was very hard, the other bird managed to guide the little bird back into the nest.

Ari asked her grandmother, "Why did the other bird help the little bird?"

Her grandmother smiled and said, "That's because love is an action. Love is something that you do. When you stop to help other people, that's loving them. Love is when you care about someone and help them, even if

it's uncomfortable, hard, or scary. It's about being there for someone and making them feel happy and safe. The other bird loved the little bird, so she worked hard to keep him safe."

Ari thought about this for a moment and then said, "I love you, Grandma." And gave her Grandmother a very tight hug.

Mountain Challenge

Just north of the Kingdom of Mertina there was a big green mountain named Mount Serenity. At the bottom of Mount Serenity was a little village called Serenity Village. And in Serenity Village, there was a little girl named Matilda. Matilda was very sporty and loved to hike and climb. She was very curious and adventurous. Her village was along the summit path to Mount Serenity. Clouds gathered at the peak, enticing Matilda to one day discover its secrets. She needed to see

what she could see. So one sunny Sunday afternoon, Matilda packed her hiking supplies, laced up her boots, and off she went.

As she started at the bottom of Mount Serenity, Matilda noticed all the beautiful plants surrounding her. Sequoia trees towered over, casting a cool shadow to the forest floor below. The trees felt ancient to her. The smell of the trees surrounding her always put Matilda at peace. She took in a deep breath and kept going. She needed to see the top.

As she climbed towards the top, Matilda noticed the scenery beginning to shift. The trees grew thinner and thinner. In their place, she saw short, woody shrubs. In the rocks, she could see delicate little mountain flowers. The air felt different up here. Every breath, she didn't get quite as much air. So she reminded herself to take small steps and deep breaths. She pressed onwards.

At the midpoint of the mountain, Matilda reached a massive boulder field. Everywhere she looked, she could see big rocks with only the most daring of small plants growing out of the cracks. Now it was time for rest. Matilda took a sandwich out of her backpack and enjoyed her lunch. As she sat and ate, she could see all of the Mertina kingdom expanding in front of her eyes. She could see the Castle and the Town below it, and even the shining sea.

After lunch, it was time to make it to the top. But getting there was proving difficult. Matilda had to climb over the rocks. It was quite difficult, as the air was very

thin. Suddenly, tears wells up in Matilda's eyes. Had she gone too far? Could she make it? She didn't know.

Just as she was about to

give up because she was tired and scared of going that far, she heard a soft, comforting voice calling out to her. It was her mother's voice. Her mother had followed her secretly and had been watching her climb up the mountain from afar. She had been worried about her daughter and decided to follow her to make sure she was safe.

Matilda was surprised and relieved to see her mother and tears of joy filled her eyes.

Matilda's mother took a handkerchief out of her pocket and wiped Matilda's tears away. "There, there, darling, you're doing great. Look how far you've made it!" She pointed to a clearing Matilda hadn't noticed before, and there was a rocky path to the peak! "I always believed in you," said her mother, "I just wanted to see it for myself."

Together they continued the climb, and her mother

held her hand, guiding her through the difficult parts. When they finally reached the top, Matilda was overjoyed and proud of her achievement. She hugged her mother and thanked her for being there for her when she needed her the most.

From that day on, Matilda realized no matter whether she thinks about it or not, she always had the caring love and support of her parents, who would be there for her no matter what challenges she faced.

You are
never alone

Grandmother's Necklace

Once upon a time, in Castle Town, there was a girl named Lily. Lily was always comparing herself to the other little girls in the town and felt like she didn't measure up. She wasn't as pretty as Tabatha, who had long blond hair all the way down her back. She couldn't sing like Sally, who could hit all the high notes. She wasn't as smart as Samantha, who got the

highest marks in school.
Lily wasn't the best at anything in her town. Sure, she could play the flute, but not as good as Olivia. Sure, she could climb trees, but not as well as Terry. She would often look at the other girls in the town and wish she was more like them. She thought they were all smarter, prettier, and more talented than she was.

Her grandmother saw Lily crying in her room, so she gave her a beautiful necklace. It was a delicate chain with a small ruby pendant in the shape of a heart. Lily loved the necklace and wore it every day. The other girls would compliment her special necklace, and it made Lily feel special. Maybe she wasn't the best at anything, but no one else had a special necklace like Lily.

One day Lily was climbing a tree to play her flute to the birds. This was a taller tree than she had ever climbed before, but she saw Terry climb this one yesterday, so now she had to. As She climbed higher and higher, the necklace caught on a branch and it broke. The chain snapped and the charm fell all the way to the ground.

Lily instantly stopped her climb and scrambled to find the necklace. The charm was still in one piece, but she couldn't wear it anymore. Lily was devastated. She loved that necklace and felt like it was a symbol of her

worth. Without it, she didn't feel pretty or special. She went to her grandmother in tears, expecting her to be upset too.

But her grandmother simply smiled and said, "Oh Lily, I know this is really sad. That necklace was a symbol of my unique love for you. But still, it's just a necklace. You still have the love that it represents. When I hear you playing your flute from the trees, it makes my heart shine just like that ruby, because you're the only one who does that.

"But Olivia plays better!"
"So? You're the only one who plays it from the trees."
"But Terry climbs trees better!"
"So? She doesn't play the flute in the trees. Being you isn't about being the best at everything. It means you have your own unique set of skills and experiences that make up you. And I still love you, with or without that silly necklace."

Her grandmother's words stuck with her, and she began to realize that her worth wasn't based on external things like her appearance or possessions, or even being the best at anything. She didn't need to prove to anyone she was special, she realized that she just was. She always was.

Over time, Lily started to accept herself. She realized that everyone has their own unique strengths and weaknesses, and that's what makes us all special. She began to focus on her own talents and interests and stopped comparing herself to others. She asked Tabitha to teach her how to braid her hair. Lily began to sing with Sally, and she would harmonize when Sally would hit the high notes. Lily asked Samatha to help her study.

Lily even formed a treetop flute band with Olivia and Terry. Once she stopped competing to prove she was the best, she realized just how special her connections

were to her friends. Lily stopped feeling so sad all the time and instead appreciated everyone for how talented they were.

The broken necklace became a symbol of her journey toward self-acceptance. She even made it into a charm that she tied to her flute as a reminder that her worth came from within, and not from external things.

You are special
and loved just
the way you are

19

Ants Never Give Up

Once upon a time, a little girl named Andrea and her father decided to go on nature walks together. They frequently went for walks together, but that time on their walk, they saw a group of ants trying to carry a big crumb of bread up a steep hill. Andrea and her father watched fascinatedly as the ants tried and failed, over and over again.

"Father, we should help them!"

"No, Andrea. Don't interfere. Just watch."

"But we're so much bigger! We can help them."

"Before you help them, first observe to see if they really need help."

Andrea huffed and puffed, but she trusted her father. The ants surrounded the crumb to lift it. Other ants would stop in the places the crumb fell before to catch it. Each time they tired, they got a little higher with the crumb. After numerous attempts, the ants got the big crumb up the hill. It looked like a miracle to Andrea.

"See Andrea? Even though the ants face many obstacles, they never give up. Let me tell you a story. Back in the old days, they still used elephants in the

circus. Do you know how they tamed the mighty elephant?"

"No Father, how?"

"They stole the elephant away from its family when it was young, and they chained it to a post. No matter how hard the elephant tried, it could not break free. He grew up in the circus, longing for his family. Even though he was a mighty elephant, he still believed the chain could hold him back."

"Oh, that's so sad!" said Andrea. Her father continued the story, "Well, one day he met a tiny little ant. The ant asked him what such a mighty elephant was doing in the circus. The elephant told the ant that he was chained, and couldn't break free. The ant asked the elephant if he had tried breaking free now that he was big and strong."

"So what did the elephant do?"

"The elephant laughed at the ant. The ant challenged the elephant to try again. So the elephant pulled in the chain that once held him, and it snapped as if it were frayed twine. The elephant thanked the ant before running back to the jungle to find his family. Andrea, do you know why I'm telling you this story?"
"No."

"The moral is, sometimes people give up after one attempt, just like the elephant who believed he couldn't break free. But if he had kept trying and never given up, he can overcome obstacles and succeed. Just like the ants."

Never give up

Science Experiment

Maria grew up near the port of Rutolia. It was a town near the ocean where boats would come into every day. Maria was extremely curious and liked to explore the beaches. Every day, she would bring back things for her mother to experiment with.

Her mother was a brilliant scientist. She would frequently take Maria on trips to the Bazaar to see what kind of wonders came in from across the ocean. Maria's mother liked to spend long nights in her laboratory, inventing new things for the people of the town.

Sometimes Maria and her mother would do experiments. Maria said her mother would one day unravel the mysteries of the universe.

Maria's father was a skilled builder. He and his team built many of the boats for the merchants of Rutolia. He would let Maria look at his blueprints for new boats.

Maria loved her father more than anyone else in the world. They did everything together. Maria's father loved to spin her around and say "That's my little girl!" and Maria's heart would swell.

But one day, a powerful governor

had heard of Maria's father's great skill. He needed a fleet of boats of his own and Maria's father would be rewarded handsomely. But he would have to be away from his wife and Maria for a whole year. They decided it would be best for the family to take the offer, and he gave Maria a big hug at the pot before he sailed away for a whole year.

Maria tried to stay strong. Still, his absence weighed heavily on Maria. The world around her became gray, lacking the color it once held. She felt like everything was always going wrong and that she couldn't handle it anymore. Her mother decided to support Maria.

"Maria, come here. I want to do a science experiment with you,"
"I don't feel like it. I'm sad."
"Please Maria, this is an experiment to help you understand your feelings."

Maria sighed but agreed. Her mother set up three clear

glass jars on the kitchen counter. In the first jar, she placed a rubber ball. In the second, she placed some loose tea leaves, and in the third, she left some water alone. Then she boiled a kettle of water.

"Ok Maria, I'm going to pour boiling water into each jar. Your job is to take notes. Please observe what happens when I do this."

As the water was poured in, the rubber ball bounced around. The tea leaves swirled and scattered. The

water remained calm.

Her mother had a sly smile. "Now dear. I want you to examine the contents of each jar."

Maria approached the laboratory table, her gaze falling upon the three glass jars lined up in a neat row. She couldn't help but wonder where her mother was going with this. What did boiling water have to do with feelings?

"What am I looking for, Mama?" she asked, her voice slowly replacing sadness with curiosity.

"Observe closely, my love," her mother replied, a hint of anticipation in her voice. "Take note of any changes you see."

Maria carefully picked up the first jar, feeling the softness of the rubber ball within. "The rubber ball has softened," she observed. She pressed it between her fingers, the once hard rubber now would change shape in her hand. "It feels a lot more flexible than before."

A smile dared to reach across her mother's face, but she quickly pulled it in. "Good job, Maria. The ball has indeed undergone a transformation. It is now Maria was starting to wonder, She moved on to the second jar, peering inside at the swirling mixture of water and tea leaves. "The tea leaves have turned the water into tea," she remarked. She noted the subtle change in color. She took a whiff of the jar, "Now it smells nice."

Her mother nodded. "Well observed, my dear. You're a great lab assistant. The tea leaves released their flavors

and colors into the water. Now it's an infusion. The water didn't change the leaves, the leaves changed the water."

Maria's sadness faded. Now she was intrigued. She turned her attention to the third and final jar. The water inside remained unchanged. "But this jar, Mama," she said, a hint of confusion in her voice, "the water looks just the same as before. Nothing seems to have happened."

Her mother had a gentle smile gracing her lips. "Ah, what an observation, my little scientist. Sometimes things not changing are just as important as things changing," she

explained. "In this case, the lack of change shows that the boiling water did nothing to the regular water. It remained unaffected."

"Maria," her mother began, her voice gentle yet filled with wisdom, "these three objects all were exposed to the same boiling water. How have the objects in these jars responded differently to the same situation?"

Maria nodded, her gaze shifting between the three jars. "Ok let's see. The rubber ball softened. Now It's squishy. I can change its shape with my hand and I Couldn't before. The tea leaves didn't react like the ball. Instead, they changed the water. And now I'm looking at the water in the third jar, and I can see it has not changed at all."

Her mother smiled, Maria was on to something. "That's correct, darling. These three different objects have way different reactions to the same boiling water. Now,

imagine these are different people facing hard times. Just like different things, different people react differently. Now here's why people are special. We have the power to choose how we respond to difficult situations in life. It's a lesson that goes far beyond these jars."

Maria's face finally began to soften. For the first time since her father left, she felt a small spark of curiosity

igniting her mind. "What do you mean, Mom?"

Her mother took a deep breath, collecting her thoughts. "When faced with challenges or unexpected circumstances, we have options. Some choose to become softer and more malleable, like the rubber ball. This allows people to be flexible and grow in the face of adversity. Some people are like tea leaves. They use their experiences and knowledge to change the world around them. They use situations as opportunities for personal growth. And even still, some people choose to remain unchanged, like the water in the third jar."

Her mother continued. "Maria, life presents us with various challenges. It's in how we choose to approach them determines our personal growth and resilience. Remember, my dear, that you have the power to become softer and wiser. You can choose to be infused with new experiences. Or you can decide to remain unchanged. Embrace the challenges, for they give us opportunities to decide who we become."

"So what's the best way to be, mother?" Maria asked with wonder in her voice.

"Well, darling, it's up to you. What do you think is the best way to respond to the situation we're dealing with right now? We both miss your father so, so much. What do you think is the best way to respond?" Her mother waited, listening for Maria's answer.

Maria thought long and hard. "Well, I want to be like the tea leaves, but I don't think I'm strong enough yet. I guess I'll be more like the ball for now."

"That's ok darling," her mother said as she pulled her in for a hug, tears welling in Maria's eyes, "it's ok to be soft. I'm here for you. All your friends are here for you. Right now you're soft, and when you grow up you'll be strong like the tea and make hard situations better for everyone around you."

Maria nodded, feeling a newfound sense of empowerment. She looked at the three jars once more, contemplating the choices before her. From that moment forward, she understood that even though living without her father for a year was hard, this was a profound opportunity for growth. She would embrace his spirit and memory with an open heart and a determined spirit.

Maria realized that she can try to change her attitude to some of the things happening and change her life for the better. By the time her father came home, she had made her own transformation. She was once a timid little girl who clung to her father's side. Now, she stood tall and spoke with confidence. Maria's father was so proud of the young woman she had become.

You choose your attitude

Exercising Princess

Not far off the coast of Rutolia was Draco's Nest Island. It was a small island with a towering mountain jutting out of the center. You couldn't see the top of the mountain, for it was always shrouded in white, puffy clouds. Legend had it, Vadir, the dragon of Draco's Nest Island lived on top of the mountain.

But that never mattered much to Sophia. She was the princess of Draco's Nest Island. Sophia was a beautiful little girl with bouncy chestnut-colored curls and bright

green eyes. Every day, her parents would tell her how she'd need to climb all the way up and receive the dragon's blessing to one day take her place as Queen of the island.

Secretly though, Sophia didn't want to do that. She didn't like climbing or scaling mountains. Everyone told her how she'd one day be queen, but she didn't want that. You see, Princess Sophia had a secret that made her different from the other princesses. The other princesses spent their days learning skills like horseback riding and archery. Sophia loved nothing more than lazing around her castle and not lifting a finger.

In the mornings, Sophia would have the servants bring her breakfast on a silver tray. When she was finished, the maids would clean it up. The ladies in waiting would then dress Sophia. Then she would saunter down to the castle library. She would sit on the comfy chair in the library and read. She would tell everyone

she was reading about History and Politics– but she was secretly reading comics instead. She loved looking at bright pictures of a brave little girl who tamed dragons. Although Sophia loved her leisurely life of reading Dragon Tamer comics, she felt like something was missing.

Her Father, King Mudlo, worried for Sophia. He noticed Sophia wasn't nearly as active as the other Princesses he saw when he traveled to the other kingdoms. He worried for Sohia's health. Her mother worried as well. Would she be able to ascend the mountain when it was her time to become Queen?

One day, Spihia became very ill. She didn't have the strength to get out of bed. Her skin had grown very pale. Her servants placed her on her balcony so she could enjoy the sunlight. Her father called the royal doctor for help.

The doctor examined the princess and realized that her illness was caused by her laziness. However, the doctor had told her many times before that her laziness would make her sick. This time, he decided to try something different.

"Oh no!" the doctor exclaimed, "it's a curse!"
"What do you mean?" asked Princess Sophia.
"Come, let me show you." The royal doctor led Princess Sophia down to the throne room, and showed her a golden statue of Vadir, the dragon of Draco's Nest Island. It had been turned around. "You see? The golden statue is out of place. You need to pick it up and turn it back."

Sophia tried to lift it,

but she was far too weak. She called for the servants, but the doctor stopped her.

"This is a magical illness," the doctor scolded, "having someone else move the statue won't lift the curse."
"Oh no, what can I do?" cried Sophia.

The doctor gave her a pair of big, shiny balls and told her, "Princess Sophia, these are magic balls. You have to swing them in your hands for half an hour in the morning and evening. This will help you move the statue and become healthy."

Sophia did as she was told and swung the magic balls every day. At first, she hated it. It hurt to lift something so heavy. She didn't like feeling sweaty. Even after it all was over, her arms still hurt. But she didn't want to be sick anymore. She wanted to move the statue and lift the curse, so she kept trying even when she didn't like it.

Within a few weeks, she started feeling better and better. She was amazed at how something so simple had made her feel so much better. She started enjoying walks around the beach of the island. She even joined in with some other children for a beach volleyball game. Before, she never would have been so brave. But now she was easily playing active games.

Soon, it was time for Sophie to try once again to lift the statue in the throne room. She had her parents and doctor watch her, lest she fail and the curse grow stronger.

However, this time, lifting the golden statue of Vadir

was quite easy.

Sophia went to thank the royal doctor and asked him how he had cured her. The wise doctor replied, "Princess, this is only the first part of the treatment. Needed exercise to grow strong enough for your final challenge. Now you must take this grappling hook and get all the way up to Vadir's nest. He is waiting." The doctor handed her a long rope with a claw on the end.

Sophie gulped but now was not the time to be afraid. She knew all along that one day she would need to do this, and now she was strong, it was also time to be brave. She took the grappling hook and went to her room. After a few deep breaths, she donned her climbing pants and boots. She no longer asked her servants to dress her, it seemed silly.

Princess Sophia approached the foot of the cliff leading up to the nest. This was not going to be easy. Her heart raced with fear, but also excitement. The towering rock

face loomed above her. She couldn't see the sun behind it. She took a deep breath, gathered her courage, and swung her grappling hook just like the magic balls the doctor gave her.

It sailed through the air easily. All that swinging really was worth it. The hook found a steady hold, and Sophie started climbing up. Soon, she found a ledge to rest and gaze out onto the ocean. She saw the world in a way she never had before. Before her world was confined to the small world inside the castle. But now the world was much bigger. Here on the cliff, the wind whistled through her hair, carrying the distant echoes of birds and rustling leaves. It was magical.

It was time to keep going. She had to go meet Vadir, and Vadir was all the way up at the very top. She tossed the grappling hook through the clouds. She couldn't see the top, but she knew she had to be close. As she climbed Sophia's arms ached. Her legs trembled, but she refused to give up. By now Sophie was determined.

She didn't want to just read about dragon tamers anymore, she wanted to be one.

After what felt like an eternity of climbing, Sophia finally reached the clouds. They felt cool and crisp and as she looked out she could no longer see the ocean, only white. She kept going. Finally, she poked her head through the clouds. She could see the very top of the cliff!

Once she got to the top, she couldn't believe her eyes. Vadir, the golden dragon of legend, was standing right in front of her. His scales shimmered in the sunlight.

"You have done well, young Princess," said Vadir "I shall now grant you my blessing to take your rightful place on the throne of the island."
Then the dragon shed a single tear made of light, which floated into Sophie's hand and became a gem. It was a Dragon's Tear, a jewel granted to only the rightful ruler

of the island. Now that Sophia had it. She would go on to be a strong and dutiful queen.

But for now, it was time to go tell her parents and her new friends all about her adventure. Sohpia was no longer the lazy princess, she was a strong and happy young girl. Sophia had learned an important lesson about the importance of physical activity and the value of hard work. She promised to keep swinging her magic balls every day and to stay healthy forever.

EXERCISE GIVES US THE STRENGTH TO ACCOMPLISH OUR DREAMS

Money for Carnival

Mia lived in Clockburg, a small town a few miles to the east of Castle Town. In the center of Clockburg, there was a giant clock whose bells you could hear throughout the whole town. Every year, the town had the Carnival of Spirits, where people would wear beautiful masks, eat carnival foods, and ride carnival rides.

The Carnival of Spirits brought people from all of Mertina to Clockburg. Mia loved the Carnival of Spirits, every year she would wear

her family's forest spirit mask. However, now that her little brother was 7, it was his time to be handed down the family's mask, and Mia was to purchase her own.

But Mia had a little problem. She had no money to buy a new mask. Every time she received money as a gift, she would spend it on many different things, like toys or comic books or candy. She would never bother to save her money at all.

One day, Mia's best friend Ava was walking with her to school.

"I can't wait for the carnival!" said Ava, "But I need a new mask for it. My little sister got my old one."
"Oh yeah, me too," Mia replied.

Ava lit up, "We should go mask shopping together! The Joyful Mask Seller should arrive in three days with all kinds of masks from all over Mertina. We can pick some

out together!"
"That sounds like a lot of fun."

Mia was very excited to go to the Carnival with Ava, but when she checked her piggy bank, she realized she didn't have enough money to buy a new mask, much less the tickets for rides and games.

Feeling sad, Mia asked her mom if she could give her some money. Her mom replied, "I give you a weekly allowance. You always spend it. You could have saved

for a new mask if you really wanted it. Money is not just about spending. It's also about saving for the things you really want."

Mia thought about what her mother said. She remembered all the afternoons she bought candy instead of putting it in her piggy bank. She knew if she had put that

money away, she could get a mask and still have money for the carnival.

But that money was now gone, so she'd have to do something else. She came up with a plan. She decided to sell lemonade near the entrance gate to travelers coming to see the festival.
Mia worked all next day, squeezing lemons, mixing sugar, and pouring the lemonade into cups. People would come in, thirsty from their travels, and be delighted to see little Mia selling ice-cold lemonade. Many were so grateful for

the refreshment, they even gave her tips. By the end of the day, she had earned enough money to buy a mask for the carnival and even had some money for rides.

The next day, Mia was extremely happy and proud of herself. She and Ava went to the Joyful Mask Seller to pick out some new masks. Mia chose a bunny mask with floppy ears. Ava decided she wanted the mask of the fox. Now that they had their new masks and some pocket money, they were ready for the carnival.

At the carnival, Mia and Ava had a blast. They rode the roller coaster, played games, and ate cotton candy. They went around guessing who was who in their masks. Mia decided she was going to spend the money she earned that night.

Finally, she had her last coin left.

"Want to buy a raffle ticket?" asked Ava.

"Sure, why not?" Mia replied.

They bought their tickets and waited beneath the clock tower. They found a place where they could look at everyone's beautiful masks and still hear the numbers being called out. Surprisingly enough, they called Mia's

number! She won a bunch of prize money.

"Do you want to spend it on more cotton candy?" asked Ava. "No, We've had enough. Let's watch the fireworks and go home.

When she got home, Mia put her prize money in her piggy bank. From that day on, Mia learned that money is not just for spending. You have to earn it, and it's worth saving. She felt proud of herself for coming up with a solution for having a mask. Furthermore, she was excited to see what she could do with her new saving habit. With her and saving, her piggy bank would grow bigger and bigger.

Save, spend, earn, and enjoy money

Lucky Butterfly

Iris was another girl living in Serenity Village, the small town at the foot of Mount Serenity just north of the Mertina Castle. She loved spending her free time in her garden, tending to her beautiful flowers. The other little girls didn't like the dirt or the bugs, but Iris understood how important these were for the flowers to grow. She loved every little insect with all her heart, except the ones that tried to eat her flowers.

One day, while she was tending to her flowers, she saw something very sad. There was a butterfly with a broken wing lying on the ground. Its wings were bright shades of blue, yellow, and pink. Usually, seeing these butterflies made Iris very happy. But sadly, one of the butterfly's wings was a little bent, making it hard for it to soar and dance in the gentle breeze. The butterfly looked sad and helpless. Iris could not bear to see the poor creature suffering.

"I'll help you," She said as she carefully picked it up and brought it inside her home.

Iris decided she would take care of the butterfly until it got better. She went to her dollhouse and found a little bed.

"This will be a cozy bed for you, little friend," said Iris. Every day, Iris gave the butterfly water and nectar. She played soft music in her room to keep it calm. She even kept a little bouquet of flowers near its bed, so the butterfly wouldn't forget its home in the garden.

The butterfly slowly started to recover. After one day, it began to crawl out of its bed. On the second day, it looked up longingly at the flowers. It would try to flutter its wings, but they were still too weak. Iris would gently encourage it, saying, "Don't worry, little one. You'll fly again soon!"

When the weekend rolled around, Iris's friend Emily came to Iris's house. Emily was surprised she hadn't seen Iris all week. Normally, they would play after school together before Iris went home to tend to her garden. Lately, Iris just went straight home after school. Emily suspected Iris had a secret, but she didn't know

what. But fortunately, Iris had left her doll at school, so Emily had a reason to investigate. Emily knocked on the door to be greeted by Iris's mom.

"Hey, is Iris home? Emily asked.
"Yes, she is, but I think she's busy…" Iris's mother replied.
"That's alright," said Emily, "I just came by to give Iris her doll back. She left it at school."

"Oh, ok, you should go give it to her."

Before Iris's mom could say another word, Emily was quickly walking down the hall to Iris's room. Emily was going to get to the bottom of this.

Emily flung the door to Iris's room open and caught her red handed. There was Iris, reading a bedtime story to a sick little butterfly. Emily was amazed.

"Oh, Iris! What happened to the butterfly?" Emily asked.

Iris looked up and smiled sadly. "Hello, Emily. This poor butterfly hurt its wing. It can't fly anymore."
Emily felt very sad for the poor little butterfly. "Is this why you haven't been playing with me after school?"
"Yes, I've been coming home early to take care of this butterfly." Iris replied.

Emily had an idea. "I want to help too, Iris. I'll take care of the butterfly when you're at school." Iris was happy to have Emily's support, and they started taking care of the butterfly together. Together, they would help the butterfly heal, reminding it that it was not alone in its journey to soar once more.

Every day, Iris and Emily tended to the butterfly with love and care. They brought fresh flowers, checked the wing, and whispered encouraging words. They watched as it grew stronger, hoping for the day it would spread its healed wings and fly high in the sky once again.

As days went by, Iris and Emily grew closer, and the butterfly became stronger. One day, when Iris and Emily were playing with the butterfly in the garden, it suddenly flew up into the air. Iris and Emily were overjoyed to see it finally fly. The butterfly circled around them and then flew away, leaving them with a sense of accomplishment and happiness.

From that day forward, Iris and Emily remained the best of friends. They would often think of the butterfly and how they took care of it together. They discovered that being kind and helping others, even tiny creatures like butterflies can bring so much joy. It can bring special people close to you, make friendships stronger, and make you feel fantastic. Knowing the butterfly's life changed because of them made Iris and Emily feel happy, even on sad days.

Helping others brings joy to yourself

True Friendship

An amazing girl Aster lived in Castle Town. Aster had a best friend named Rosie. They had been friends since they were little and did everything together. They went to the same school, played in the park, and even had the same hobbies. Aster and Rosie had a deal with each other: if one of them ever wanted to try a new thing, the other would try it with them.

One day, while they were playing in the park, they

saw a new girl sitting alone on the bench.

"We should go say hi," said Aster.
"But we don't know her," said Rosie.
Aster shrugged. "So? She might be nice. Besides, you know our deal with new things. I want to try talking to her, so you have to try with me." Rosie nodded. They approached the new girl together. Rosie spoke first.

"Hi, I'm Rosie, and this is Aster. What's your name?"
"I'm Mia, I'm new in town so I don't really have any friends," said the new girl.

"It's nice to meet you Mia, "Aster said, "where are you from?"
"Well, my family just moved here from Clockburg," replied Mia.
Just then, Rosie's face lit up. "Oh, I love Clockburg! Every year my family makes a trip for the Carnival of Spirits!"
"Yeah, that's Clockburg," Mai said as she blushed and looked at her feet. She was clearly very shy.
Aster had an idea. "We should show you around the playground," she insisted.

"Please do… I have no idea what's around here," said Mia. Aster and Rosie were very welcoming while they showed Mia around the park. They played together, laughed together, and had a lot of fun. They showed her how to play marbles, and Mia promised to show

them a new card game tomorrow.

As the days went by, Mia started to open up to Aster and Rosie. She told them that she was finding it hard to adjust to the new town. She missed her old best friend Ava and was feeling lonely.

Lily and Rosie listened carefully and decided to help her.
"Hey Mia," said Rosie on the playground one day, "Aster's family is coming over to my house for dinner tomorrow night. You should come too."
"I'm not sure…." Mia said back.

"Well, ask your mom," Aster said, "it's a really fun time, we all play games. It would be fun to have you there."

"Ok," said Mia.

That night, Miai asked her mother if she could have dinner over at Rosie's house, and her mom said yes! Mia was so excited to be spending time outside of school with Rosie and Aster.

Dinner at Rosie's house was lovely. Mia brought her family, and Aster brought hers as well. Mia got to meet Aster's sister Lily, who could play the flute. Rosie's mom cooked a big, tasty feast with all of Mia's favorite food. After dinner, the three youngest girls went off to Rosie's room.

"Here Mia, let me show you something," said Rosie as she reached into her toy box. She pulled out a mask. It was the face of a beautiful woman with bright pink hair.

"This is the fairy mask I wear when we go to the Carnival of Spirits in Clockburg!" said Rosie.
Mia looked at it and began to tear up.
"Don't cry," said Aster, "she didn't mean to make you sad."
"No," said Mia, "I'm just so happy someone in this town knows about it."
All three girls hugged. For the first time since she moved to Castle Town, Mia finally had friends again. Aster and Rosie were happy to have found another friend they could both be close to.

From then on, they started spending every weekend together. Aster and Rosie would take Mia to the library and the swimming pool and even introduced her to

their other friends. Mia started to feel much better, and her sadness disappeared. She was happy to have found such wonderful friends in Aster and Rosie. And they were happy to have helped Mia.

The three girls became inseparable. They would play together, study together, and do everything together. As they grew older, they made a trip every year to see the CLockburg Carnival of Spirits. Aster and Rosie were thrilled to meet Mia's old friend Ava, and all the children of Clockburg. They'd buy cool masks from the Joyful Mask Seller, play games, and make memories.

They knew that true friendship meant being there for each other, no matter what.

As they grew they faced many different challenges, but they always stood by each other's side. No matter whether times were good or bad, they faced it all together. They discovered that true friendship means being there to support each other through thick and thin, and they cherished their bond. It's important to be kind, welcoming, and open-minded towards new people, just like Aster and Rosie were to Mia.

True friendship means being there for each other

You are UNIQUE

Out in the fields outside of Castle Town there was a mysterious and magical forest called Wayward Woods.

Once, a little bird named Robin was born there. Every morning, she would find her perfect branch in her favorite spot to watch the sunrise and sign to the brilliant sun as it displayed its colors. Robin was always inspired by all the colors of the sunrise.

Even though she was a small and simple bird, she had a big dream: to be as beautiful as the peacock. She

admired the peacock's colorful feathers, which shone in the sunlight. More than anything, she wished that she could be as glamorous as he was.

One dewy morning, Robin saw the peacock shaking off the morning dew, showing off his feathers. The dew illuminated his already brilliant feathers. When he fanned his tail, it was like a million divine eyes gazed

upon her. The show was stunning. She couldn't help but compare her own plain brown feather to his shiny blue and green feathers and feel inadequate. She thought to herself, "My brightest feathers are just a muddy red. Why can't I be as beautiful as the peacock? What's wrong with me?" As she was lost in thought, she heard something above her. "Hoo-hoo, Robin, look up here!"

The wise old owl Ebera appeared before Robin. Nobody in the Wayward Woods knew how old Ebera was, but he was definitely older than all the other animals. According to the legend, Ebera was as old as the largest tree in the center of the forest. The owl had lived for many years and had seen many birds struggle with the same thoughts as Robin.

"Why are you so sad, little Robin?" asked Ebera.

"Nothing," Robin insisted, "it's stupid."

"Seems like you're rather upset, little bird," Ebera stretched his wings as he spoke, "Even if it is over something stupid, it's wise to talk about it. Don't bottle up your feelings."

"I want to be as beautiful as the peacock, but there's no way I can measure up," Robin admitted.

"Oh Robin," said Ebera, "everyone is beautiful in their own way."

"Well, I want to be beautiful in the peacock way!" Robin shot back.

"I think it's time for you to learn the peacock's secret. Follow the peacock to the center of the

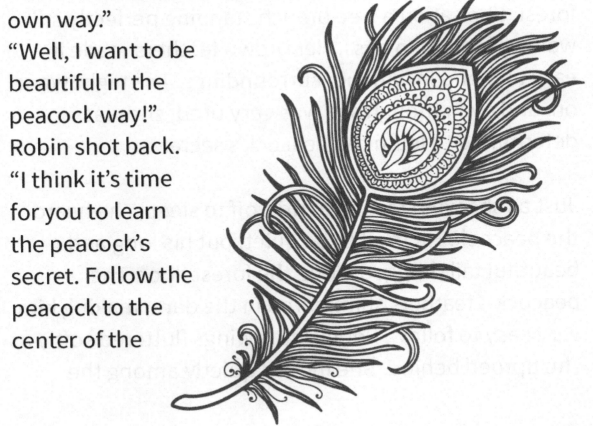

woods at midnight. It's a full moon tonight, so your path will be lit. You'll learn something important about him."

Robin decided she'd listen to Ebera and follow the peacock that night. Maybe she'd learn his beauty secret and be able to take it for herself. Either way, the full moon was worth being out for.

That night, Robin followed the peacock through the forest. She sat on a tree branch standing perfectly still, waiting for him to pass. Her brown feathers made it easy to blend in with her surroundings. The night went on, and even though she was very tired, she was determined to learn the peacock's secret.

Just as she was starting to drift off to sleep, she heard the peacock. He tried to be quiet, but his long and beautiful tail dragged along the forest floor. The peacock's feathers shimmered in the dark, making him very easy to follow. Robin's tiny wings fluttered softly as she tiptoed behind. She moved quietly among the

trees, barely making a sound. The night sky twinkled with stars, guiding them on her secret journey. Robin longed to sing the beauty of the night sky, but she did not dare risk the peacock finding her.

The peacock led her through twists and turns in the forest. There was a thick haze in the woods, making it easy to get lost, but Robin could see the shimmer of the peacock's feathers. She pressed onwards.

Eventually, they came to a clearing in the brush. She could see other peacocks. There was even a little

campfire. There, they beheld a breathtaking sight. The full moon was shining brightly above. Robin nestled behind a bush, watching in awe as the peacocks stood together majestically in the moonlight. All of their feathers sparkled, reflecting the moon's gentle glow. Robin felt a flutter of excitement in her little heart, knowing she had discovered something special.

"Brothers in beauty," the peacock said to his fellow fowl, "tonight is the night of the full moon. You know what that means."
"What???" What's your secret?" Robin whispered to herself.
"It is time for us… to SING!!!" the peacock stated proudly.
Another peacock piped up. "Let us praise the beauty of the moon!"

Robin closed her eyes and opened her ears. She was trembling with excitement "I've never heard the

peacocks sing before!" She thought to herself, "They must sound as beautiful as they look."
The peacocks all lifted their beaks towards the moon, and let out their cry.

"AWRAK!!!! AAWRRAAKK!!!! AAAWWWWRRRAAAAAKKKKKK!!!!" they shrieked. Robin quickly covered her ears and opened her eyes. She wondered what could possibly be making such a racket. She saw the peacocks all screaming at the moon and decided to leave.

On her way back, the owl Ebera greeted her once more.
"So did you learn the secret of the peacocks?"
"Uh, I don't think I did. I didn't stick around long enough to see the whole thing." Robin replied.
"Why not?" Eberea asked as he tilted his head.
"Because it was noisy!" Robin continued, "I had no idea such a beautiful bird could make such an ugly sound!"
"Hmm… really? Because I know a little brown bird who

may not have very shiny feathers but sings a beautiful song to the rising sun every morning." Ebera leaned in towards Robin even more. Robin blushed.

"...You mean me!" Robin asked shyly.

Of course I mean you, Robin" Eberra replied, "you are already beautiful and unique. You may not have the colorful feathers of the peacock, but you have a beautiful voice that can sing the sweetest melodies. The peacock does not have such a gift."

Then it hit Robin. How could she be so foolish? She had been so focused on what she didn't have that she had forgotten to pay attention to her natural gifts. She started to sing proudly. Her voice was so beautiful that the peacocks came over to hear the beautiful music of the night. Hearing Robin's beautiful singing, they began to dance and sway in the moonlight. Together, they created a dance that made the whole forest shimmer.

From that day on, the peacock and Robin became good friends. They learned that everyone is unique and special in their own way. Together, they realized that it's important to appreciate and make the most of what you have.

Robin learned that true beauty comes from within. Even though her feathers weren't shiny, she was beautiful just the way she was. And if she ever doubted her own inner beauty, all she had to do was look around her and let the beauty come through in her song.

There is no
one like you

Epilogue

Dear girl,

As you come to the end of this book, I want you to take a moment and think about all the amazing stories you've just read. Which one did you like the most?

I hope these stories have inspired you to believe in yourself, to be kind to others, and to embrace your own unique qualities. Remember that you are special just the way you are. You have so much to offer the world!

You may encounter challenges and obstacles in your life, but I want you to remember that you have the strength and courage to overcome them.

As you move forward, I encourage you to continue reading, learning, and growing. Keep exploring the world around you, and never be afraid to be yourself. You have the power to make a difference in your own life and the lives of those around you.

Thank you for reading this book, and I hope it has left you feeling inspired and empowered to be the amazing girl that you are.

With love and admiration,
Lily M. Green

Made in the USA
Las Vegas, NV
16 August 2023

76071288R00050